For my best friend Roz – L.B.
For Marion – R.B.

BLOOMSBURY
CHILDREN'S
BOOKS

First published in Great Britain in 2003 by Bloomsbury Publishing Plc
38 Soho Square, London, W1D 3HB

Text copyright © Lisa Bruce 2003
Illustrations copyright © Rosalind Beardshaw 2003
The moral right of the author and illustrator has been asserted

A CIP catalogue record of this book is available from the British Library
ISBN 0 7475 5916 3

Printed in Singapore by Tien Wah Press

1 3 5 7 9 10 8 6 4 2

Fran's Friend

Lisa Bruce and Rosalind Beardshaw

BLOOMSBURY
CHILDREN'S
BOOKS

It was a lovely sunny day.
Fred wanted to play.

Come on!

But Fran was busy.
"Not now, Fred," she said. "I want to make something."

Can I help?

"I need some paper. I want
to make something special."

Fred found the paper.
"Not the newspaper,
Fred."

Oops!

Fran found some paper and cut a big square
shape out of it.
Bits of paper fell on to the floor like snowflakes.

What a mess!

"Not that kind of brush, Fred. I need a paintbrush. I am making something very special."

Fran swirled the water in the jar.

Hey, I'm wet!

Fred was fed up. He looked at the leaves
dancing in the wind.
They could have such fun chasing them.

He took his lead to Fran.

"I can't go out yet," said Fran as she started to paint. "I am making something very special for my best friend."

Your friend?

Fred sat down under the table. He sighed.
Drips of water fell on to his nose. Drops
of red and green paint fell on to his fur.
He didn't care.

I wish Fran would play with me

Oh goody!

At last Fran jumped up. She ran to the door.
"Only one thing left to do," she said.

Fred brought his ball but Fran went out.
She left Fred behind.

Fred slunk slowly into his basket.
He hid his head under his paw.

It's not fair

"Where are you, Fred?" called Fran.
Fred didn't answer.

Fran held out a card.
"Here you are, Fred," she said.
"I've made this for you."

To the best friend in the whole wide world x

Thanks, Fran!

"Come on, Fred, let's go out and play."

To the best friend in the whole wide world x

Whoopee!

And they did!